Circus Train

WRITTEN AND ILLUSTRATED BY Jos. A. Smith

HARRY N. ABRAMS, INC., PUBLISHERS

Acknowledgments: My thanks to Howard Reeves, who should be declared a national treasure.

Designer: Darilyn Lowe Carnes

The artwork for each picture is prepared using watercolor on paper.
The text is set in 17-point Cothral.

Library of Congress Cataloging-in-Publication Data

Smith, Joseph A.
Circus train / written and illustrated by Jos. A. Smith.
p. cm.
Summary: After moving to a house in the country, Timothy wonders how he will make any friends, but his problem is solved when he finds an imaginative way to rescue a stranded circus train.
ISBN 0-8109-4148-1
[1. Circus—Fiction. 2. Railroads—Trains—Fiction.] I. Title.
PZ7.S65215 Ci 2001
[E]—dc21 00-42152

Published in 2001 by Harry N. Abrams, Incorporated, New York

Printed and bound in Hong Kong

Harry N. Abrams, Inc.
100 Fifth Avenue
New York, N.Y. 10011
www.abramsbooks.com

For my wife Charissa
and for Kari, Joe, Emily, and Andrea
for their contribution
to keeping the circus going in my life

Artist's Note

Circus Train started from an old photograph I found of a yard-crew posing in front of a steam engine in a train yard. The picture inspired a series of fantasy train watercolors. One of these was of the shadow of a passing circus train, which in turn was the seed for this story. There was a time when the idea of "running away to the circus" was very much alive for all children who wanted to be part of a world that they saw as full of mystery and wonder. I have purposely combined the nostalgic look and mythical feel of the circus and its animals and players with modern depictions of children—for instance their dress—to make the story meaningful and relevant for children today.

The pictures come entirely from my imagination. My illustrations begin as loose pencil sketches on heavy watercolor paper. I work over the pencil sketch in transparent watercolor, refining the drawing with my brush. I know what feeling and quality of light I want and how the image will fit on the paper, but I never know what the finished picture will look like until I see it in final form. I continue to add details until it feels right to me. Some of these pictures took a week or more to complete. At the end, I often add colored pencil to make a color richer.

—J.A.S.

The morning after Timothy's family moved into their new home, his parents drove to Yonderville to go shopping. Timothy had all morning to get dressed, so he sat on the back porch in his pajamas with Curly, listening to the birds discuss worms with each other. "How will I ever meet any friends when we live way out here?" he wondered.

Just then Timothy heard a distant sound. It grew louder. It was not the sound of birds singing or the house creaking as the sun warmed its night-chilled boards. There were clanks and rumbles, a long hissss followed by a moment's silence. Then voices.

Timothy and Curly raced to the front of the house to see what was happening and froze in disbelief. "A circus train," Timothy whispered to Curly. "But Dad said trains don't run on this old track." He charged off through the weeds for a closer look with Curly a few steps behind.

“What’s going on?” panted Timothy. “Why did you stop?”

“We don’t know,” said a worried clown. “We’re waiting for the engineer to tell us. Our circus is supposed to be in Yonderville today.”

Timothy had to see for himself what was happening at the front of the train, so off he went.

What a train this was! The more he saw, the better it got.

Worried voices could be heard among the grunts and roars of animals. Horns mixed with drum rolls drifted off to settle into silence among the weeds.

Curly followed Timothy out onto the bridge, where a man sat in the cab of the engine. "What's wrong, Mister?" Timothy asked, pulling gently on the toe of his huge shoe.

"The bridge is out. I must have switched onto the wrong track," the engineer moaned, "and my engine can't back up. We're stuck." He climbed down and led them to the front of the engine.

“That’s Yonderville over there, but it might as well be a thousand miles away.” The engineer gazed sadly down between his long green shoes.

Timothy stared across the empty space and scratched his nose thoughtfully with his bubble wand. A lion roared. An elephant trumpeted. Suddenly the boy's eyes lit up. "Mister—er. . ."

"Carrot Top."

"Get the engine ready, Mr. Top. I'll be right back." Timothy turned and disappeared into the steam.

At the elephant car, Timothy slid back the bolt and the heavy door rumbled open. He screwed up his courage and tugged on the nearest tail. "Come on, guys," Timothy said. "We have work to do." He tugged harder.

The elephant backed carefully out into the sunlight. Soon Timothy was leading a parade of elephants toward the rear of the train. Everyone stopped what they were doing to watch.

At each car, Timothy placed an elephant. He took its trunk in his hands and pressed it carefully against any opening he could find. Then Timothy took a great gulp of air and blew with all his might. The elephants caught on immediately.

With each blast of elephant breath the cars got bigger and bigger. Soon the entire train looked like a billowing string of balloons that lifted off the tracks on each passing breeze, then settled down again as soft as a sigh.

Timothy led the elephants back to their cars at a trot. "Everyone get on the train," he shouted. "Somebody find Captain Von Boom. Next station Yonderville!"

The Captain stepped through the steam and bowed. Timothy threw Von Boom the end of a rope, shouting instructions as he ran to the engine where he tied the rope's other end. With a mighty BOOM and a billow of smoke Von Boom was launched high into the air out over the fallen bridge with the train in tow.

VON BOOM

The cannon's thunder echoed across Yonderville and beyond, bringing everyone running out onto the streets and lawns. Timothy's parents, in the market's parking lot, could not believe their eyes as the train soared over the awestruck town.

VON BOOM

The train settled slowly to earth at the fairground. Bull's-eye, a perfect shot!

That evening music blared, trapeze artists tumbled through the air, and the circus was under way. Timothy's mother and father clapped proudly as Timothy rode an elephant into the center ring.

"Timothy, you have saved the circus," Carrot Top announced. Timothy smiled shyly as everyone cheered.

When the applause ended, Timothy climbed down from the elephant and took a seat with his parents for the big show.

The following morning Timothy sat on the back porch tossing a ball to Curly. "If only you *really* knew how to play baseball." He sighed. Suddenly Timothy heard a sound. Then a familiar voice: "Come on, we're almost there."

"Carrot Top!" With a WHOOP of glee, Timothy and Curly raced to the front of the house.